Donated 4/20

God
got a dog

CYNTHIA RYLANT and MARLA FRAZEE

God
got a dog

BEACH LANE BOOKS
New York - London - Toronto - Sydney - New Delhi

These poems were originally published
by HarperCollins without illustrations
as part of a larger collection entitled
God Went to Beauty School © 2003.

BEACH LANE BOOKS

An imprint of Simon & Schuster Children's Publishing Division

1230 Avenue of the Americas, New York, New York 10020

Text copyright © 2003 by Cynthia Rylant

Illustrations copyright © 2013 by Marla Frazee

For information about special discounts for bulk purchases, please contact Simon & Schuster Special Sales
at 1-866-506-1949 or business@simonandschuster.com.

The Simon & Schuster Speakers Bureau can bring authors to your live event. For more information or to
book an event, contact the Simon & Schuster Speakers Bureau at 1-866-248-3049 or visit our website at
www.simonspeakers.com.

Book design by Marla Frazee and Ann Bobco

The text for this book is hand-lettered.

The illustrations for this book are rendered in graphite pencil and gouache on Strathmore paper.

Manufactured in China

10 9 8 7 6 5 4 3 2 1

Library of Congress Cataloging-in-Publication Data

Rylant, Cynthia.

[God went to beauty school]

God got a dog / Cynthia Rylant ; illustrated by Marla Frazee. — First Beach Lane Books edition.

pages cm

Revised edition first published by HarperCollins in 2003 under title: God went to beauty school.

Summary: "Newbery Medalist Cynthia Rylant and two-time Caldecott Honor medalist Marla Frazee
imagine a God inspired to go out and experience human things"—Provided by publisher.

ISBN 978-1-4424-6518-3 (hardcover) — ISBN 978-1-4424-6519-0 (ebook) [1. Novels in verse.

2. God—Fiction.] I. Frazee, Marla, illustrator. II. Title.

PZ7.5.R95Go 2013

[Fic]—dc23

2013005577

God woke up

And He was groggy,
so He got a nice cup of coffee
and went to sit
under an apple tree.
He sat there
 drinking His coffee,
listening to the birds,
when all of a sudden
it hit Him.
He was happy.
God was HAPPY!
And He wished there
 was just someone to see it.
He'd gotten such a bad rap
all these years
for being pissed off
all the time.
And He really wasn't.
Maybe a little CRANKY.
But here He was,
 HAPPY.
 Mellow yellow.
The birds were singing
and He was at peace.
Buddha told Him it
could be this way,
but He'd never really
believed it until now.

Life really was easier,
            sitting under a tree.

God went to beauty school

He went there to learn how
to give a good perm
and ended up just crazy
about nails
so He opened up His own shop.
"Nails by Jim" He called it.
He was afraid to call it
Nails by God.
He was sure people would
think He was being
disrespectful and using
His own name in vain
and nobody would tip.
He got into nails, of course,
because He'd always loved
hands —
hands were some of the best things
He'd ever done
and this way He could just
hold one in His
and admire those delicate
bones just above the knuckles,
delicate as birds' wings,
and after He'd done that
awhile,
He could paint all the nails
any color He wanted,
then say,
"Beautiful,"
and mean it.

God got in a boat

And said, "Wow."
She'd never actually
floated in a boat, though
She'd seen people
out on the water and
told Herself She'd have
to try that someday.
Water had always bored Her
until She started seeing
people having fun on it.
So one day She got in a boat,
said Wow,
and headed out across the lake.
And the whole world looked different.
She couldn't get over it.
It didn't look anything like
it looked from the sky
or from the ground
or even from inside a whale,
which She'd tried once or twice.
She sat in the boat
and was surprised how
much sense it all made.
All the little houses
and all the green trees
and all the tidy cities
and all the sky and all the land,
it all made sense.
She was surprised.
Because, really,
She'd just been winging it.

God made spaghetti

And She didn't have a ceiling
so She tried to make it stick
to Jupiter
but that just
vaporized the noodle,
so God decided to
HAVE FAITH it was cooked
al dente.
She filled up a big bowl
and got Herself a
piece of sourdough
and a copy of
The New Yorker
and God
had supper.
And She would actually
have liked somebody
to talk to
(She didn't like eating alone),
but most people
think God
lives on air
(apparently they've not noticed
all the *food* She's created),
so nobody ever
invites her over
unless it's Communion
and that's always
such a letdown.
God's gotten used
to one plate at the table.
        She lights a candle
                anyway.

God went to the doctor

And the doctor said,
"You don't need me,
You're God."
And God said,
"Well, you're pretty good
at playing me,
I figured you'd
know what the
problem was."
So the doctor
examined Him.
She couldn't find
anything wrong
except a little
skip in God's heart.
"Probably nothing,"
she told God.
"But eat more fish."
God sighed.
He was hoping
for more than that.
Maybe an antibiotic.
Or a shot.
He knew about that
skip in His heart.
He knew it was nothing
fish would cure.
The skip had started way back,
when He first heard
that some people
didn't believe in Him.
It scared Him.

Still does.

God got arrested

But they didn't
know it was Him
because He had on
His disguise.
It was His guy-disguise.
He was actually
pretty proud of it.
It had a tattoo
around the belly button
(which hurt!).
Anyway, He got arrested
because He got
into a fight in a bar
when somebody said
something about
Jesus Christ except
not in a good way
at all.
Might as well have
insulted God's mother
(now that's a whole
other story), because
God—who was only there
because He liked
the jukebox—
lost it.
And his anger erupted like
the wrath of...
Oh, *right*. Never mind.
Just be careful
dropping names
in Kenny's Tavern.
Might be next to a relative.

God took a bath

With Her clothes on.
Her robe, to be specific.
Why did She do this?
She was shy,
that's why.
A little self-conscious
about Her body.
God wasn't always
this way.
She used to be free as a bird,
running stark naked
everywhere.
She never thought
about bodies at all.
Then these things
started coming back to Her:
The whole misunderstanding
with Adam and Eve.
Then circumcision.
Then talk talk talk
of everybody being made
in Her image.
Until She got afraid
to look in a mirror.
Everybody had such
high expectations
and now She was
a little insecure.
Could be She was flabby.
Love handles on God
would have to be HUGE.

So She kept Her robe on.

God went skating

He loved it.
He wasn't very good at it.
He fell twenty times.
But God always
bounces back.
"Cool!" said God
as He whooshed
past the old ladies.
He felt
invincible.
(He knew He WAS
invincible
but He didn't
always feel that way.
Not every day.)
God made some other
friends on
skates.
God thought
they were
WAY COOL.
He was proud
of them.
Proud that they
flew their spirits
down the alleys
and the boardwalks
and the streets
like angels.
    They were, you know.
        And they
            hadn't forgotten.

God caught a cold

And He was such a baby.
He NEVER caught colds.
He loved to brag about it.
And now here He was:
snot nosed.
It's hard to be
authoritative
with a cold.
It's hard to
thunder
"THOU SHALT NOT!"
when it comes out
"THOU SHALT DOT!"
Nobody takes Him
seriously.
And besides,
He wanted some comic books
and juice
and somebody to be
nice to Him.
He called up His
old friend
Mother Teresa.
He asked her to
come over and see Him.
He asked could she
bring some comic books.
And of course she did.
Mother Teresa loves
all who suffer.
Even God.
Maybe Him a little more.

God wrote a book

No, not *that* one.
Everybody thinks She
wrote *that* one,
but She didn't.
She's a better writer
than that.
Those guys just
went on and on
and did they
bother to edit?
No.
But wouldn't you know,
you mention a name
and you're in.
So they said,
"*I* didn't write it,
God wrote it."
A sure way
to get out of revising.
But God wrote
Her *own* book.
She wrote it for
one little boy.

Just one.

She read it to the boy
at bedtime
because the boy couldn't sleep.
So God read him a book.
The boy grew up. He became a writer.
Which one?
Not telling.

God got cable

And for a week
watched nothing but.
Didn't see the comet.
Didn't see the hurricane.
Missed that baby
being born entirely.
Just watched cable.
Funny thing is,
He liked it.
He knew He wasn't
supposed to.
All those girls
crying about their
boyfriends.
All those track meets.
All that
soap and toothpaste.
He liked it.
Couldn't help it.
Then Gabriel came
over with a deck of cards
and next thing you know,
they've played poker
four weeks straight,
Gabriel's beard nearly
as long as God's
and corn chips all over the place.
And what God decided was that
He liked not *cable*,
not *poker*,
but a break.
Every now and then,
even God needs a break.

God found God

It was the *weirdest* thing.
God got all religious
on Herself.
She was looking for
something to do
so She went into this
church in Boston.
One of those churches
from the 1800s that
likes to consider
itself *old*.
(This always gives
God a good laugh.)
And She was all by Herself
and it was quiet
like you wouldn't believe,
and up to the sky
went these beautiful rafters,
and all around Her
were these beautiful stained glass windows
and everybody was praying.
All the people in the pictures,
all the statues,
all the angels in the room,
were praying.
God knew better than to look
at any of the crosses.
She was still trying to figure
that all out.
But She knew that She
had actually found a Holy Place.
So She dropped a coin in the
Building Fund box, before She went away.

God got a desk job

Just to see what it
would be like.
Made Her back hurt.
God's always had a
bad back anyway—
the weight of the world
and all that.
She thought *Her* job was tough,
till She sat at a desk all day.
It was torture.
She could feel the Light
inside Her grow
dimmer and dimmer
and She thought that
if She had to pick
up that phone
one more time,
She'd just start the
whole Armageddon thing
people keep talking about.
(Not Her idea, not Her plan,
but in a pinch, She's
sure She could come up
with something.)
The only thing that got
Her through to the
end of the day was
Snickers bars.
She ate thirty-seven.
Plus thinking about the Eagle Nebula
in the constellation Serpens.

 That helped.

God wrote a fan letter

To this country music
singer He liked.
God *rarely* writes fan letters,
so He figured the singer
would make a
big deal out of this.
He figured He'd get
an autographed photo
or something.
But she never wrote back.
Nothing.
So He wrote her again.
And He signed it
"God. *Really*."
Nothing.
Finally He wrote
one last time.
He told her how much
He liked her singing
and how He had her
concert video, which
He played over and over,
and how, if she wanted,
He could answer her prayers.
Well — one at least.
And finally, *finally*
she wrote back.
And she said,
"Dear God, I pray
you will get a life."
Well, thought God.

Just what did she mean by that?

God went to India

To see the elephants.
God adores elephants.
He thinks they are
the best thing
He ever made.
They do everything
He hoped for:
They love their children,
they don't kill,
they mourn their dead.
This last thing is
especially important
to God.
Elephants visit the graves
of those they loved.
They spend hours there.
They fondle the dry bones.
They mourn.
God understands mourning
better than any other emotion,
better even than love.
Because He has lost
everything He has
ever made.
You make life,
you make death.
The things God makes
always turn into
something else and
He does find this good.
But He can't help missing all the originals.

God got a dog

She never meant to.
She liked dogs, She'd
liked them ever since She was a kid,
but She didn't think
She had time for a dog now.
She was always working
and dogs needed so
much attention.
God didn't know if She
could take being needed
by one more thing.
But She saw this dog
out by the tracks
and it was hungry
and cold
and lonely
and God realized
She'd made that dog
somehow,
somehow She was responsible
though She knew logically
that She had only set the
world on its course.
She couldn't be blamed
for everything.
But She saw this dog
and She felt bad
so She took it on home
and named it Ernie
              and now God...

has somebody
   keeping Her feet warm at night.

CYNTHIA RYLANT's novel *Missing May* was awarded the Newbery Medal, and her novel *A Fine White Dust* received a Newbery Honor. Cynthia lives in Portland, Oregon.

Two of MARLA FRAZEE's picture
books received a Caldecott Honor for
illustration: *A Couple of Boys Have the Best
Week Ever*, which she wrote, and *All the
World* by Liz Garton Scanlon. Marla lives
in Pasadena, California.